Hattie B Magical Vet

The Unicorn's Horn

CLAIRE TAYLOR-SMITH

Illustrated by Lorena Alvarez

PUFFIN BOOKS

Published by the Penguin Group

Penguin Books Ltd, 80 Strand, London WC2R ORL, England

Penguin Group (USA) Inc., 375 Hudson Street, New York, New York 10014, USA

Penguin Group (Canada), 90 Eglinton Avenue East, Suite 700, Toronto, Ontario, Canada M4P 2Y3
(a division of Pearson Penguin Canada Inc.)

Penguin Ireland, 25 St Stephen's Green, Dublin 2, Ireland (a division of Penguin Books Ltd)

Penguin Group (Australia), 707 Collins Street, Melbourne, Victoria 3008, Australia
(a division of Pearson Australia Group Pty Ltd)

Penguin Books India Pvt Ltd, 11 Community Centre, Panchsheel Park, New Delhi – 110 017, India

Penguin Group (NZ), 67 Apollo Drive, Rosedale, Auckland 0632, New Zealand
(a division of Pearson New Zealand Ltd)

Penguin Books (South Africa) (Pty) Ltd, Block D, Rosebank Office Park,
181 Jan Smuts Avenue, Parktown North, Gauteng 2193, South Africa

Penguin Books Ltd, Registered Offices: 80 Strand, London WC2R ORL, England

puffinbooks.com

First published 2014

001

Text and illustrations copyright © Penguin Books Ltd, 2014
Story concept originated by Mums Creative Content Ltd
Illustrations by Lorena Alvarez
With thanks to Claire Baker
All rights reserved

The moral right of the copyright holders and illustrator has been asserted

Set in 14.5/24pt Bembo Book MT Std
Typeset by Jouve (UK), Milton Keynes
Printed in Great Britain by Clays Ltd, St Ives plc

British Library Cataloguing in Publication Data
A CIP catalogue record for this book is available from the British Library

ISBN: 978–0–141–34464–5

www.greenpenguin.co.uk

MIX
Paper from
responsible sources
FSC® C018179
www.fsc.org

Penguin Books is committed to a sustainable
future for our business, our readers and our planet.
This book is made from Forest Stewardship
Council™ certified paper.

To Jamie,

Love you everything

xxx

To Cod,

Love you to the moon and back

xxx

Rumbling
Volcano

Troll
Bridge

Fairy Forest

Rainbow
Waterfall

Ancient
Desert

Hidden
lake

Frozen
Merlakes

Contents

Chills and Charms

Hattie Bright's teeth were chattering as she stood at the side of the swimming pool. She'd just swum five lengths of breaststroke and her wet costume felt cold now that she was out of the water.

'Right, girls,' said Mrs Riley, the swimming teacher. She grabbed three yellow rings from beside the pool and hurled them into the water. 'Today at Swimming Club we'll be working towards our lifesaving badge. The next thing I need you all to do is dive down and grab those rings from the bottom of the pool. Who would like to go first?' she asked the shivering line of girls in front of her.

'I love diving,' whispered Hattie's best friend, Chloe, into her ear, 'don't you?'

Hattie nodded in agreement. She was really looking forward to getting her lifesaving badge. Hattie loved helping other people almost as much as she loved helping poorly animals at her parents' vet's practice. She went to the practice whenever she could and

everybody knew she wanted to be a vet herself when she was older.

A loud splash announced that the first person had dived in without even volunteering aloud. Sure enough, Hattie soon spotted Victoria Frost, probably the meanest girl at school, climbing elegantly out of the far end of the pool, with barely a hair out of place and not a wrinkle in her shimmering pink swimming costume. Victoria's two best friends, Jodie and Louisa, dived in next before anyone else had the chance. They scooped up the rings easily, then returned them to Mrs Riley and followed Victoria to the side of the pool, where she was now sitting on a bench, her long legs stretched out in front of her.

'OK, just you two to go then,' said Mrs Riley, throwing the rings back in the pool, but not before raising a disapproving eyebrow at Victoria and her friends. 'Hattie, you dive in first. Chloe, you can go after her.'

Hattie moved to the very edge of the pool and placed her feet together, curling her toes over the edge of the smooth cream tiles, but when she looked into the rippling blue water she felt a flutter of nerves in her tummy. She could only just see the yellow rings at the bottom of the pool, even though she'd watched

Mrs Riley throw them in seconds ago. Hattie took a deep breath, placed her arms in a neat curve above her head and prepared to dive in.

'Is everything OK, Hattie?'

The voice made Hattie jump. It took her a moment to realize it must have come from Mrs Riley, who was now striding towards her, a look of curiosity on her face. Hattie wondered how long she'd been standing there, waiting to dive. It felt like it had only been a moment or two, but then she spotted Victoria and her friends pretending to look at their watches and mouthing fake yawns.

'Doesn't Swimming Club finish at half past four?' she heard Victoria whisper loudly to Louisa. 'I do hope Hattie makes it into the water before teatime!'

Hattie felt herself blushing at Victoria's mean words. *I can do this!* she told herself, stretching her arms as high above her head as she could. But then why could she feel herself shaking from her fingertips to her toes? During half-term Hattie and Chloe had gone to the new theme park outside town and had been on every ride, including the Terrifying Tumbler, twice! Hattie hadn't been scared even once then, so why was she so nervous now? Hattie felt as if she was frozen solid.

Chloe stepped forward and slipped her arm round her friend's trembling shoulders. 'Hey, Hattie,' she said gently, 'why don't we hold hands and jump in together? You grab one ring and I'll get the other.'

Hattie knew Chloe was just trying to be kind, but it was no use. All she wanted to do was get away from the water. She mumbled a quick 'sorry' to Mrs Riley and, with the sound of Victoria and her friends' sniggers ringing in her ears, she ran away from the pool and into the changing room.

Tears filled Hattie's eyes as she grabbed her towel and wrapped it round her shivering body. She'd just finished drying herself when Chloe ran into the changing room and threw her wet arms round her friend.

'Are you OK?' Chloe asked. 'Sorry I took so long. Mrs Riley insisted I do my dive before I came to find you.'

'I . . . I don't know what happened,' said Hattie. She tried to smile and put on a brave face. 'I just felt so scared when I looked into the water. I couldn't do it.'

'Don't worry, Hattie,' said Chloe. 'It's only a silly dive. I know how brave you are usually.

Remember that time you rescued the kite I got
for my eighth birthday? There was no way I
was going to climb up that huge tree to get it,
but you went straight up so I wouldn't get into
trouble with my mum.'

Hattie knew it was true. She hadn't been scared at all then, but that didn't explain why she'd felt so nervous by the pool – especially now she was two years older.

'Victoria and her friends will never let me forget this.' Hattie shook her head sadly. 'I bet they go on and on about it at school tomorrow!'

Chloe hugged Hattie even tighter. 'Who cares what Victoria thinks?' she said, although she knew Hattie probably cared quite a bit. 'Victoria's just horrible. You don't need to prove how brave you are to her – or her copycat friends.'

Hattie wasn't convinced. 'Shouldn't you get back to the pool, Chloe?' she said as she took off her swimming cap. 'Mrs Riley will wonder where you've got to, then we'll both be in trouble.'

'Well, if you're sure you're OK?' replied Chloe uncertainly.

Hattie nodded weakly as Chloe headed back to the pool with a small wave.

With her clothes on and hair up in a ponytail, the last thing Hattie did was put on the pretty silver bracelet that she'd got for her tenth birthday. The two crystal charms on it – a simple star and a tiny dragon – swung daintily as she fastened the delicate clasp. It was only when

Hattie lifted her arm to wriggle the bracelet down that she realized both charms had started to glow. At first the clear crystal shimmered gently and within seconds the charms became a

warm yellowy orange, and Hattie was sure it could mean only one thing.

Forgetting all about the failed dive and Victoria's sneering, Hattie grabbed her bag and made her way out of the changing room. In the foyer she peered through the large windows and was relieved to see that her mum was parked just outside, early and already waiting to pick Hattie up.

Hattie bounded out to the car and quickly climbed in. There was something she needed to do.

Back to Bellua

On the way to their village Hattie sat quietly in the back of the car, deep in thought. She let down her hair to hide the fact that she was sneaking peeks at her bracelet. She couldn't deny that the star and dragon charms were definitely still shining brightly.

Once they arrived home Hattie's mum opened the front door and they stepped inside, Hattie dumping her bag full of damp swimming stuff in the hall.

'Is everything all right, Hattie?' asked Mum.

'It's just you were so quiet in the car. Was Swimming Club OK today?'

'Oh yes, Mum, it was fine,' replied Hattie. 'It's all that swimming – I'm exhausted!'

'I bet you are,' agreed Mum as Hattie gave her a quick hug. 'Why don't you go and lie down in your room for a bit while I start making tea? Dad won't be home from work for at least an hour and Peter's eating at a friend's today.'

No big brother here to bug me, thought Hattie. At least the rest of her day was starting to look up.

Hattie went to her room and shut the door. Relaxing on her bed, she looked at the charms on her bracelet again. She was sure they were glowing even more deeply now.

Smiling, Hattie remembered the first time she'd seen that happen and how she had been more than a little alarmed!

The bracelet and star charm had arrived on her tenth birthday, wrapped in brown paper along with a battered old vet's bag. There had been no note to explain who had sent it to her – or why. Hattie had put on the pretty bracelet anyway, and soon after that the charm had begun to glow.

At first she'd been puzzled but had soon realized that the charm matched the shape of the lock on the vet's bag. The moment she'd pressed the charm against the lock, the bag had sprung open – and that's when Hattie's world had changed forever! Upon peering into the bag, she'd fallen into the Kingdom of Bellua – a magical land of mythical creatures, from unicorns and fairies to mermaids and dragons.

Hattie reached under her bed to grab the scruffy vet's bag, hidden away from Peter's prying eyes. She laid it on her lap, feeling the scuffed brown leather under her fingers. Taking a deep breath, she gave it a long look, knowing it would lead her back to the land where she'd experienced the most incredible adventure of her life.

Hattie grinned with excitement at the thought of returning to Bellua. She hoped she would see her new friend again, a little pink dragon called Mith Ickle whom she'd helped on her last visit. Mith Ickle had given her the

dragon charm as a thank-you gift, and it reminded Hattie of their friendship.

However, Hattie also had a huge responsibility in Bellua – and a difficult task ahead. She'd inherited the role of Guardian from her Uncle B, and now all the creatures of Bellua relied on her to cure them when they were sick – and to protect them from Ivar, King of the Imps. The evil Imp King planned to steal magical powers from the creatures so that he could become the all-powerful ruler of Bellua. He'd already successfully stolen Mith Ickle's voice, because a dragon's song would give him the ability to send his enemies to sleep. There was no question in Hattie's mind that King Ivar wanted even more magical powers – and he didn't care about the creatures he harmed to get them.

The glowing charms on Hattie's bracelet were a sure sign that King Ivar had struck again and that another creature was in need. Her tummy flipped as she remembered how Immie, a mean imp who served King Ivar, had tricked Hattie into going to the Winter Mountains. As long as Ivar sought power, Immie would keep trying to stop Hattie from succeeding as Guardian. Shaking off her worries, Hattie knew that she was ready to take on whatever challenges were thrown at her this time. She had to be brave for the creatures of Bellua!

Hattie held the bag and, with only the tiniest hesitation, she placed the star charm carefully against its lock. Would it have the same effect as last time?

She didn't have to wait long to find out. The lock clicked open and the dull leather of the bag began to turn sparkly silver. Soon after, two letters started to emerge, glowing against the silver with a soft purple light: *H* and *B*.

Hattie couldn't help smiling at the sight. There was no doubt about it, the bag was meant for her: *H* for Hattie and *B* for Bright.

She slowly opened the bag and peered inside, wondering, *Will this take me to Bellua?*

Her question was answered immediately as she found herself tumbling down, down and down . . .

A Creature in Need

Hattie couldn't control the tumble any more than on her first visit to Bellua, but this time she was determined not to land clumsily on her bottom. She reached out both arms, hoping to grab on to the large stone table in the centre of the cave. But it was no use! With a final *whoosh*, Hattie felt herself sweep past the table, her fingertips scrabbling at its edges as she toppled on to the hard cave floor.

With a sigh, Hattie sat up and was delighted to see a tiny pink dragon peering at her from round the side of the table. Hattie couldn't stop a huge grin from spreading across her face.

She'd so hoped Mith Ickle would be in the cave to greet her. She also knew that, with her friend at her side, she was sure to be brave enough for any challenge that King Ivar or Immie might throw her way.

'Mith, you're already here!' Hattie cried.

The little dragon smiled back. Her wings

were fluttering quickly but gently, showing
that she was as happy as Hattie at their reunion.

'But are you OK?' asked Hattie. 'Do you
need my help again?'

Mith Ickle shook her head. 'No, Hattie, it's not me. There's another creature who needs you this time.'

Hattie had missed the dragon's beautiful melodic voice. Mith Ickle could barely whisper when Hattie had first met her, but then Hattie had found and used the incredibly rare sunray flower to cure her friend. When Mith Ickle was able to speak properly at last, it had been like hearing a hundred-strong choir singing all at once.

'I'm so glad it's not you,' replied Hattie, slowly picking herself up from the floor while Mith Ickle looked on with a toothy grin.

Now Hattie was upright again, Mith

Ickle flew over and landed on her friend's shoulder. Hattie was comforted by the warmth radiating from Mith Ickle's pink scales and the friendship reflected in the dragon's shining eyes.

'So who do I need to help? Has King Ivar taken another magical power?' asked Hattie.

Without waiting for a reply, she started searching the glittering cave. Tiny crystals embedded in the rock walls gave the cave its sparkling and magical appearance, but that was only a hint of the magic that lay outside.

Over on the far side of the cave, Hattie saw a portrait of Uncle B. It reminded her that they shared the same distinctive streak in their

hair, and a tiny star-shaped birthmark that identified them as the true Guardians of Bellua.

Hattie was so proud to have inherited this

role from Uncle B. Curing and helping creatures in need was all she'd ever wanted to do – whatever the creature: puppy, kitten, dragon or fairy!

After looking between the dusty bottles on the shelves, under the stone table and around the sparkly crags in the walls, she began to doubt whether the creature was in the cave at all.

Hattie turned to her friend and asked, 'Mith, where am I going to find who or what I'm looking for?'

The little dragon smiled before saying in her sweet rich voice, 'Let me show you!'

Hattie followed Mith Ickle to the wooden door at the back of the cave, a swirl of excitement growing inside her. Taking a deep breath, she opened the door to reveal the lush and colourful Kingdom of Bellua.

Everywhere, the magical land glowed and sparkled with magic. Galloping, flying and fluttering by were creatures that Hattie had only ever dreamed about. She could hardly believe that she really was here again!

Looking around, Hattie wondered if she would have to travel through Bellua to find the next magical creature in need. She looked at Mith Ickle questioningly, and the dragon nodded silently to the side. Then Hattie spotted the tip of a long spiralling horn poking out of the luscious green grass. She didn't need

to ask anything else. Mith Ickle's expression confirmed that her patient was waiting for her just outside.

Hattie walked across the velvet-soft grass, Mith Ickle fluttering beside her protectively. She gasped in surprise to find that there, nestled in the long grass, lay a majestic silvery unicorn, its face crumpled in sorrow and pain.

'It's OK,' whispered Hattie, bending down by the sad creature's side. 'You don't need to worry – I'm here to help you.'

Torn in Two

The stricken unicorn didn't say anything in reply and Hattie felt very sorry for him as he lay helplessly on the ground. His beautiful purple and silver coat was dampened by the dewy grass, and his mane lacked the deep silky glossiness of the manes Hattie had seen on the healthy unicorns she'd met on her first visit to

Bellua. The unicorn's long hair was lying in all directions. It was dull and looked painfully matted in places, a bit like Hattie's hair when she was feeling ill.

'I'm Hattie, the Guardian of Bellua,' said Hattie quietly. 'I'll do everything I can to help you get better,' she added, placing one hand on the unicorn's trembling nose and looking into his eyes. She couldn't help but notice how dim they were, as though a light mist had covered any twinkle in them. What had caused this magnificent creature to be in such a sorry state?

As if reading Hattie's mind, Mith Ickle showed her what was wrong. Swooping down

gently, so she wouldn't startle the injured
unicorn, the little dragon pointed to his
horn, which stood tall and proud on his bowed
head.

'Of course!' said Hattie in a hushed voice. 'Unicorn horns should glow. I remember seeing them lighting up the meadows of Bellua on our way to the Rumbling Volcano.'

Hattie could see that this unicorn's horn had no shine to it at all. It was a flat, grey-brown colour, as if it were made of dusty stone. Even worse than its dull lifeless colour, Hattie was shocked to discover that there was a large crack running down one side, almost splitting it in two. Hattie winced when she imagined how much it must hurt. She'd once tripped over and broken a toe and that had been painful enough, but she was sure that a broken horn, being so much bigger and full of the unicorn's magical powers, must be agony!

'I think I might be able to find a way to help fix your broken horn,' Hattie said to the unicorn, sounding more confident than she felt. 'But first let me introduce my friend, Mith,' she added, as the pink dragon settled on one of her shoulders. 'I hope you won't mind if she helps a little too.'

The unicorn smiled weakly.

'Thank you, Hattie – and Mith,' he replied, his voice low and husky. 'My name is Lunar. Themis, the leader of our unicorn herd – or 'blessing' as we call it in Bellua – told me

how you heeded his warning to avoid
the mischievous fairies in the Fairy Forest
on your first visit. Word later reached him of
your success in restoring a dragon's lost

voice. That must be you, Mith. He was most impressed and believes you to be someone we unicorns can trust.'

Mith Ickle looked at Hattie proudly.

Hattie remembered Themis well. She had been in awe of his majestic size, his gleaming bright white coat and long glossy lilac mane. It was Themis who had personally welcomed her to Bellua as the magical land's new Guardian.

Then a low groan from Lunar interrupted Hattie's memories. She was surprised to see he had pulled himself upright, though his long legs seemed a little shaky with the effort.

'I would be so very grateful if you could

fix my broken horn, Guardian,' he said sorrowfully. 'With my horn cracked in two, I have no magical powers and . . .' Lunar paused, weak from both standing up and talking.

Hattie gently stroked the unicorn's neck in concern.

'When a unicorn loses his or her magical powers, a little of Bellua's magic is lost for everyone,' said Mith Ickle, taking over since Lunar was too tired to continue. 'This is King Ivar's work again. He wants every creature to be as miserable as possible and, not only that, he's now stolen the healing power of a unicorn. This power keeps the natural world strong. The Kingdom of Bellua, from its trees to its lakes and sky, feeds off the magic of the unicorns, so that is why a little of Bellua's magic is lost when one of them is injured.'

Hattie looked around her. Had Bellua lost some of its magical sparkle already? Were the colours just a little less bright, the sky just a touch less twinkly? She couldn't be sure, but either way she knew she had to heal Lunar's broken horn.

Mith Ickle fluttered closer and added, 'Not only can unicorns heal but they can influence the weather too. We need to help Lunar get better so he can join his blessing in keeping Bellua's magic strong.'

Hattie was determined that King Ivar wouldn't have his evil way. She could see the unicorn was getting weaker and his voice wasn't as strong when he raised his head to speak again.

'Mith is right,' he said. 'It was while helping the enchanted trees of Bellua that my horn came to be cracked. A rare magical storm, not often seen in our land, had ripped a branch from an ancient twisted tree that stands just beyond the Fairy Forest. The branch was hanging by the thinnest splinter of wood, barely attached to the tree. As I prepared to use my healing power to fix it, I heard a creaking noise above me. Afraid that another storm was brewing, I glanced up and saw King Ivar, jumping on the broken branch. I realized that he intended to break it completely, but before I could stop him the branch fell and knocked me to the floor. It was only when I stumbled to my feet again that I noticed it had cracked my horn. I was in too much pain to lift my head to see where King Ivar was, but I could hear his menacing laugh as he fled. I am certain that wherever he went he took my magical powers with him.'

Listening to Lunar's story, Hattie knew she would do everything she could to heal him. However, there was one problem to start with – how to get him into the cave where generations of Guardians had healed the magical creatures of Bellua over many years.

'Do you think you can make it to the cave?' Hattie asked the poorly unicorn, pointing towards the wooden door, which was still open. 'It's really the best place to treat you.'

Lunar nodded and took a few hesitant and wobbly steps towards the entrance. With Hattie and Mith Ickle whispering encouragement, he slowly made it inside, dipping his head to avoid further damaging his horn on the door frame.

Hattie felt a twinge of nerves and excitement

that her next adventure in Bellua was about to begin.

'Now,' she said, 'let's find a way to bring back the magic in a unicorn's horn!'

The Search for a Cure

Hattie had no idea yet how she might heal Lunar's broken horn, but she knew where to start looking.

Heading towards the thick, rough stone shelves cut into the cave walls, she gazed up at the heavy red book that had showed her how to restore Mith Ickle's lost voice. The search for that cure had led her on the most amazing adventure of her whole life! She hoped that inside the book's scuffed leather covers, with its faded gold dragon-like design on the front, she would again find the information she needed for a cure.

As before, the book was balanced unsteadily on the highest shelf, surrounded by many tiny potion bottles, which had been left there by generations of Guardians before her. Looking along the shelf, Hattie couldn't help feeling a small rush of pride when she spotted a small clear bottle carefully placed at one end. It was filled with the remainder of the sunray flowers that she had gathered – the same flowers that Hattie had used to bring back Mith Ickle's lost voice.

'Do you think you could help me to get the book down, Mith?' Hattie asked, remembering how the pink dragon's tiny claws were perfect for cradling the fragile glass

bottles. 'I'm a bit scared I might break something.'

'Of course,' replied Mith Ickle, gently flying towards the laden shelf.

Hattie watched patiently and with fascination as Mith Ickle hovered back and forth, moving bottles out of knocking-over distance.

As soon as Hattie saw it was safe to lift the book from its place on the shelf, she began to climb on to the huge stone table to reach up for it. She only paused when she heard the soft voice of Lunar call her name. She looked over in surprise to see that the injured unicorn had risen to his feet and was shakily trotting to where Hattie was precariously balancing.

'Here, Hattie,' he said, crouching down and lowering his head. 'Climb on!'

Hesitating briefly to make sure she didn't knock Lunar's painful horn, Hattie climbed on to his outstretched neck. The unicorn gently nudged her into position and then slowly stood up. Hattie gasped in delight as he raised her towards the book. She reached up to grab it quickly, not wanting to put him under any more strain. She held the red leather book tightly to her chest as Lunar slowly bent back down again, allowing her to slide off carefully.

Hattie stroked Lunar's muscular neck gently, whispering a grateful 'thank you' before the

unicorn limped back to where he had been and lowered himself to the floor with a tired sigh.

Hattie had forgotten how heavy the old book was and she was glad to put it down, though a little unsteadily, on the stone table. Knowing what to do this time, Hattie lifted her wrist and carefully placed the star charm on her bracelet against the book's lock. Both the lock and the charm began to glow brightly, then, with a sharp and satisfying *click*, the thick red cover sprang open.

'Oh!' Hattie jumped as a large sheet of blank paper flew out and fluttered on to the table, but then she smiled as a detailed map of Bellua began to magically appear on it: volcanoes, mountains, paths, meadows and lakes, and many other intricate features of the magical kingdom, formed in front of her. This was the map that had helped Hattie find her way to the Rumbling Volcano on her last adventure!

Hattie carefully put the map aside and turned her attention to the first page of the red leather book. Although she had seen it happen once before, Hattie still watched open-mouthed as the title began to appear across the blank page: *Healing Magickal Beastes & Creatures*. She felt a small rush of excitement to read the words again.

However, after several minutes of flicking through the book's dusty pages, Hattie felt her heart sink. She knew the book didn't have proper sections or chapters like her books at home, but she had forgotten just how jumbled its pages were.

There were illustrations and diagrams of all kinds of magical creatures. Some of them Hattie had met on her last visit to Bellua, some she hadn't – and some she hoped she might never meet! But she couldn't find a section on unicorns *anywhere*. Not wanting to worry Lunar, who was resting wearily against one wall of the cave, Hattie silently beckoned Mith Ickle over to help.

'There doesn't seem to be anything in the book about unicorns at all,' whispered Hattie a little anxiously. 'Do you know where I should look?'

Mith Ickle shook her head, but settled down on the table next to Hattie, indicating they should look together.

'You're right,' Hattie murmured gently with a grateful smile. 'Two heads are better than one!'

Together, the little dragon and Hattie searched the worn pages, one at a time. Mith Ickle ran her tiny claws gently down columns of neat text and intricate diagrams so that they didn't miss a single thing. Then, finally, at almost the very end of the book, Hattie spotted what she was looking for. The page was entitled 'In the Unlikely Evente of Unicorne Misfortunes' and listed a handful of conditions that might require treatment.

'Thank goodness for that!' exclaimed a relieved Hattie, startling the resting Lunar.

'You've had some success?' asked the unicorn, looking hopeful.

'Oh yes,' replied Hattie. 'I'm sorry it took me so long, but it wasn't easy to find any information on healing unicorns and I'm quite new to all this and –'

'Don't worry, Hattie,' interrupted Lunar. 'The Guardian's book doesn't often mention unicorns, because we already have the power of healing. Once fully grown, a unicorn may treat the ailments of their own kind with great success. We seldom trouble the Guardians.'

Hattie wanted to tell Lunar that he was no trouble at all, that she wanted to help *all* the creatures in Bellua whenever they needed her, but Lunar hadn't finished speaking.

'There are a few conditions we cannot cure,' he continued, 'and, alas, a cracked magical horn is one of them. This is why I sought your help, Hattie. Only you can find a way to heal my horn and so restore my magical powers.'

Hattie could feel a familiar churning of nerves in her tummy as she remembered that the responsibility for this injured unicorn rested entirely with her. Lunar and Mith Ickle both looked at her trustingly, and Hattie felt, for a moment, as though she was back by the edge of the pool, waiting to dive. As Lunar's sad, dull eyes gazed into hers, Hattie knew she couldn't give away how nervous she was. With a reassuring smile, she met his gaze and pushed away those horrible feelings of doubt in her mind.

Taking a deep breath, Hattie turned again to the red book. With Mith Ickle looking over her shoulder, she searched up and down the page on unicorns. Then, right at the bottom, she spotted a tiny illustration of a unicorn curled on the ground, a large crack clearly visible in its horn.

Hattie couldn't help widening her eyes in

wonder as words written in ancient script began to fill the space next to the picture in front of her.

A unicorne with horn broken in two has too fewe magickal powers. It is said that a sicke unicorne brings sicknesse upon all of Bellua. Only a paste of magickal moonstone and rainbow water applied to the horn may bring this creature to healthe once more – and thus bring back full healthe to all of the Kingdom of Bellua.

Hattie gulped. The ancient script really brought home that it wasn't just Lunar but, to some extent, all of Bellua that was relying on her this time. If King Ivar could send creatures to sleep and control the natural world around him, then he would be very powerful indeed.

Nervously she carried on reading as a verse appeared hinting at where in the magical world the moonstone might lie:

This stone is not for all to see,
And rests beneath a special tree.
Atop a hill, in grass so long,
This tree stands tall and full of song.

So that gave her a clue to the moonstone's whereabouts, but, even after Hattie had read everything on the page twice, she still couldn't see anything about rainbow water. She began to feel a little desperate, glancing over at Lunar anxiously and hoping that he couldn't pick up on her nerves.

'Just wait there, Hattie!' Mith Ickle's musical voice echoed around the cave walls, giving Hattie a sudden glimmer of hope.

The little dragon flew to one of the shelves and clasped a small glass bottle in one of her clawed feet.

'Is this what you need?' she sang, coming back and passing the bottle to Hattie. 'It was one I moved so you could take down the book.'

Hattie held the dusty bottle up to the

sunlight that was streaming through the open
door and multicoloured rays shone like a
kaleidoscope across her face. Turning the
bottle round, with great relief Hattie could

now see that the faded label read RAINBOW WATER.

'Thank you so much, Mith!' she cried. 'That's half of the cure found. All we need to do now is find the moonstone. Now what did the riddle say? It's under a tree, on a grassy hill and it's got something to do with singing . . .'

'I have heard the music of the Singing Tree,' said Mith Ickle in her own sing-song voice. 'It filled the skies that my dragon family were flying through one starry night, but it was dark and we did not know exactly where it came from. It was beautiful, though,' added the little pink dragon dreamily.

'The melodies of the ancient Singing Tree of Bellua call out to all the creatures of our magical kingdom.' Lunar's voice was still weak, but Hattie thought she detected an element of hope.

'You know this tree, Lunar?' Hattie asked excitedly.

'Yes,' the unicorn said, his face glowing a little with obvious relief. 'It sings from the top of a hill, surrounded by the lush grass of Unicorn Meadows.'

'Unicorn Meadows? That's not far from the cave at all!' Hattie wondered at the fact that her second adventure into Bellua seemed quite simple in comparison with her first. Could it really be true?

She walked over to where the unicorn lay on the floor, breathing heavily.

'You stay here, Lunar,' Hattie said, gently stroking his matted mane. 'Rest now and we'll find that moonstone and have you cured in a flash. And, Mith –' Hattie turned to her friend – 'this time I'll watch out for that nasty Immie from the start. We're going to have to be prepared for whatever horrid surprises she comes up with. Come on, let's go!'

Hattie grabbed the map from the stone table, in case they needed it, and ran out through the wooden door into the sunny and magical Kingdom of Bellua.

A Change of Plan

Walking through the Valley of the Guardians, Hattie gazed in wonder at the many creatures that scurried and fluttered past her. Just like in *Healing Magickal Beastes & Creatures*, there were some she had been lucky enough to encounter on her last visit, but she was certain there were others that were even more weird and wonderful! Fortunately, none of them seemed too concerned by the presence of a ten-year-old girl and a small pink dragon, and before long the two friends found themselves standing under a towering silver arch. The wide arch was decorated with beautiful flowers – it was the entrance to Unicorn Meadows.

'We're here!' cried Hattie, delighted to have reached her destination so quickly.

Her joy only began to fade when she spotted a large group of unicorns standing just beyond the arch. Their elegant faces were twisted in concern as they examined a small patch of withering flowers. It looked like Lunar's injured horn was starting to affect Unicorn Meadows.

Hattie felt the now-familiar knot of nerves in

her stomach. What if she couldn't fix the horn? What if the magic of Bellua continued to weaken? Her fears shrank slightly when the biggest and grandest of the unicorns moved away from the group and trotted towards her. Hattie recognized his beautiful white coat and silky lilac mane immediately. It was Themis, the head of Lunar's unicorn blessing.

'Hello, Guardian, it is an honour to meet you again,' said Themis, lowering his head in greeting. 'We know why you are here and trust that Lunar is safe and not suffering too much.'

'He's OK, Themis, but I really want to be able to help him as soon as possible. I can't bear to see him in pain.' Hattie's brow wrinkled with worry just thinking about it.

'Yes, I can see why you have become the next Guardian,' Themis said, looking thoughtfully at Hattie. 'You possess the love for this world that your uncle has. It is your care that will protect us from King Ivar. Word has reached me that he has been angry ever since he learned that his imp servant failed to disrupt your good work on your last visit here. His fury knows no bounds and there is a rumour that he will stop at nothing now to ensure your failure as a Guardian. Should Immie fail in her task again, who knows what havoc King Ivar will wreak in his quest to stop you! Be assured, Hattie: we unicorns will help you in any way possible, but you must take the greatest care on your travels through Bellua.'

Hattie caught her breath. 'Thank you for the warning, Themis,' she began. 'Perhaps you can help me with something right now – I'm looking for the magical moonstone. I think it's under the Singing Tree of Bellua, in Unicorn Meadows. As this is your land, could you help me find it?'

'I wish I could, young Guardian,' replied Themis, shaking his head gravely. 'It is true, it *should* rest among the roots of the Singing Tree, high on a hill in our very own meadows, but a misfortune has befallen us. The magical moonstone has been stolen!'

Hattie gasped and looked at Mith Ickle in horror. The little dragon curled herself comfortingly round Hattie's shaking shoulders as Themis continued: 'Fear not, Guardian, we are not without hope. Aurora, step forward and tell the Guardian what you saw in the meadow today.'

Nudged by one of the older unicorns, a small unicorn foal stepped out from the blessing, her delicate legs wobbling slightly. Hattie thought the little unicorn was beautiful, with her silvery coat and wispy blue mane, the colour of a summer sky.

The unicorn spoke softly. 'I was dancing through the grass with my friends when I

saw someone running away from the Singing

Tree and through the meadows — a girl, I think.

I couldn't see who it was, but as she ran she

was muttering something about how nobody would ever find her near the lakes.'

'Did you see anything else?' asked Hattie, keen to find out as much as she could.

'Only some blue hair that I spotted afterwards, caught on the Singing Tree's rough bark,' replied Aurora, before retreating shyly back into the shelter of the unicorn blessing.

'Blue? That has to be Immie!' Hattie exclaimed aloud. She felt a rush of anger. *So Immie is still helping King Ivar. I won't let them get away with it!*

'We must get to the lakes,' Hattie said to Mith Ickle, who was still curled round her shoulders. The little pink dragon nodded in agreement.

'Now, where did I put the map?' Hattie frantically fumbled in her pockets, looking for the magical map, when Themis interrupted her in an urgent voice.

'Be careful, Guardian. The only lakes you will find in Bellua are the Frozen Merlakes. These lakes are home to the mermaids – creatures so ill-tempered and unpredictable in their actions that no other would attempt to enter their dwelling. Hattie, know that it *will* be dangerous there.'

'That's an awfully big risk for Immie then. She must be terribly afraid of King Ivar if she's willing to go there on his behalf,' Hattie said thoughtfully.

Themis's wise grey eyes looked troubled. 'I believe you may be right, Guardian. There are also rumours of a hidden lake – one even the mermaids won't enter. However, the only time it can be found is when the sun is highest in the sky. It is not a place to be entered in the dark – who knows what creatures lie in wait! It may be that Immie is leading you there for some other reason,' he said.

Hattie gulped. With the threat of King Ivar lying ahead, Hattie started questioning whether she really was brave enough to be the Guardian. For the first time since being in

Bellua again she thought of her best friend, Chloe, and wished she was there to give her some support.

Mith Ickle shifted nervously on Hattie's shoulder, but blew a reassuring puff of warm air in her ear.

Themis also sensed Hattie's worry. 'I can tell you no more now, Guardian, as time is of the essence if you and your dragon friend are to find the hidden lake in time. But I remind you: the magical creatures of Bellua will always help you when we can, just as you will help us, so you are not alone.'

Hattie's doubts were replaced by a surge of courage. She knew she could rely on her new friends if anything went really wrong. After all, it was Mith Ickle's dragon friends who had saved her when she had been stranded in the Winter Mountains.

Themis nodded his majestic head and rejoined his blessing.

'I wish you well,' he called, as the beautiful unicorns rose into the sky together and headed off towards the outer meadows.

As Hattie reached out one hand for Mith Ickle and felt for the map with the other, she realized she hadn't even had a chance to say goodbye.

Old Friends

'We'll have to pass through Dragon's Valley,' said Mith Ickle happily, as Hattie traced her finger around the magical map until she reached the Frozen Merlakes. 'I'll be able to introduce you to all my family and friends, Hattie.'

Hattie smiled. She'd hoped to have a chance to thank Mith Ickle's dragon friends for saving her in the Winter Mountains. But even the thought of visiting Dragon's Valley didn't take away all Hattie's nerves.

The two friends passed under the arch, away from the safety of Unicorn Meadows, and began their perilous journey towards the Frozen Merlakes. Themis's warning about Ivar and the mermaids ran around Hattie's head, but she only had to close her eyes and picture Lunar's sad face to remind herself why they had to keep going.

Hattie folded the map away once it became clear Mith Ickle knew the way to Dragon's Valley. She was happy to follow the excited little dragon as they walked through fields and woods, passing all kinds of magical creatures, from suspicious-looking trolls to inquisitive sprites.

They had just left a pretty pixie-filled flower garden when Hattie found herself facing a huge wall of rock as high as it was wide. She looked up and down it with increasing alarm. There didn't seem to be any sort of doorway or opening to pass through, or any way of going round it. Was their path to the merlakes completely blocked? What were they going to do now?

Hattie looked over at Mith Ickle, but the little dragon didn't seem concerned at all. In fact, she was flapping her wings excitedly as she swooped towards a particularly jagged section at the bottom of the wall.

'Mith! Where are you going?' Hattie asked in confusion.

'Follow me!' called Mith Ickle, beckoning Hattie with one of her long claws. 'We're here!'

Before Hattie could ask where exactly *here* was, Mith Ickle crouched down and began singing softly. Hattie couldn't quite make out the words of the song, but it wasn't long before she noticed that the jagged rocks were starting to part, revealing a doorway big enough for her to pass through easily.

'Go in, go in,' said Mith Ickle, nudging

Hattie gently on one shoulder. 'I want to show
you Dragon's Valley!'

Once inside, it was as if every dragon had
heard Mith Ickle's song announcing their arrival.

Dragons of all colours, shapes and sizes suddenly appeared, excited to see Mith Ickle and the new Guardian they'd heard so much about. Hattie recognized at least four or five of the dragons who had rescued her from the Winter Mountains. She soon spotted the large red dragon who had revealed Immie the Imp's evil plan to let her freeze there. It was this dragon who cleared his throat with a large puff of smoke and, introducing himself as Ladon, addressed the two visitors.

'Our dear friend and relative, Mith Ickle, and our most welcome Guardian, Hattie. In the rocky nook over there you will find platters of the finest fruits. We would be most honoured if you would share a delicious feast with us before your adventure takes you beyond Dragon's Valley.' Ladon raised a claw to indicate the nook.

Hattie noticed that smaller dragons had begun to fly into it, bearing plates piled high with hundreds of kinds of fruit. Although her mouth was already watering, Hattie couldn't help remembering how Themis had insisted there was no time to lose if they were to get to the hidden lake on time. Before she could say anything to Mith Ickle, she realized that the little pink dragon was already making her way there. Hattie sighed gently. She was still very grateful to have been rescued by Mith Ickle's friends and she didn't want to upset them by rushing off. Deciding they wouldn't stay too long, she ran over to join the feast.

The pieces of fruit offered by the dragons didn't look or taste like anything Hattie had

ever eaten at home. Some were sweet, some sour, and some even tasted a bit like peppermint! Even stranger was the effect the different pieces had *after* Hattie and Mith ate them. After nibbling a small purple fruit, Hattie found she couldn't stop giggling and could hardly get out the words to ask Mith Ickle what was happening.

'It's a chucklecherry,' she explained. 'Try this, Hattie – that should stop it.'

Mith Ickle handed Hattie a piece of yellow fruit filled with tiny black seeds, taking a second piece for herself. The two friends had barely swallowed it when its effects became clear.

'*Atishooooo! Atishoooooooooooooo!*' Hattie's loud sneezes were muffled by Mith Ickle's even noisier ones, each accompanied by a large puff of smoke.

'Pepper pear,' said Mith Ickle, a little apologetically, once the smoke had cleared. 'What about this one, Hattie? I think it might be a bit sweeter and it'll work much better on you than me.'

Hattie took the piece of pink fruit Mith Ickle was holding out towards her. On biting it, her tongue was immediately coated with the sweetest of juices and she was delighted to find that the sneezing stopped at once. With no other obvious side effects, Hattie couldn't work out why Mith Ickle was looking at her so intently until the little dragon gently lifted a strand of Hattie's hair and held it in front of her eyes. Hattie couldn't believe it – her hair was bright pink!

'That was a blush banana,' said Mith Ickle. 'They turn things pink, but don't worry – it wears off after a minute or two.'

Hattie thought it might have been quite fun to keep her pink hair – although she knew if the effects didn't wear off before she left Bellua she would have quite a lot of explaining to do at home!

'Time for another piece, Mith?' asked Hattie, who was now quite excited to see what exactly the next magical fruit could do. 'Let's try this one.'

'Are you sure you —' But, before the little dragon could finish her question, Hattie had grabbed a bright green berry from the platter and popped it into her mouth. 'Oh well, if you're going to eat one, I suppose I should too,' said Mith Ickle, helping herself to a berry.

It took a moment for the effect to take hold, but once it did it was inescapable.

'What is that —' began Hattie, before Mith Ickle finished the question: 'Smell?'

The two friends wrinkled up their noses. A revolting stench, like rotting rubbish, had filled the air around them.

'Oh yuck!' said Hattie, pinching her nostrils

together. 'Please tell me *that* won't last forever either, Mith!'

'No, Hattie, don't worry,' replied Mith Ickle. 'The smell will fade in a few minutes. The effects of the stinkberry are unpleasant but can sometimes be useful.'

Hattie couldn't imagine when it might be useful to turn your whole body into a walking whiff, but she was glad to discover that the effect wasn't permanent.

It was only when she noticed that the platters were almost empty that Hattie wondered how long they had been enjoying their unusual fruit feast. She squinted upwards and was shocked to see that the sun was already quite high in the sky.

She turned to Mith Ickle and whispered urgently in her ear: 'Didn't Themis say we needed to arrive at the merlakes when the sun was at its highest to be able to find the hidden one? We've stayed too long. We have to get going before Immie escapes with the moonstone!'

Mith Ickle looked at Hattie in dismay. 'Can't we stay just a little bit longer?' the little pink dragon asked, her musical voice cracking.

Hattie felt guilty. She loved her adventures in Bellua but she missed her friends and family, so she knew a little of what Mith Ickle must be feeling.

'I'm sorry, Mith,' Hattie apologized, trying

not to look at the disappointment on her little friend's face. 'We'll come and visit again soon – I promise.'

Mith Ickle's eyes filled with tiny crystal tears and Hattie didn't know what to say. She hated to see her friend looking so sad.

Luckily Ladon, seeing what was happening, stepped forward at that point to bid them goodbye.

'Farewell, Mith Ickle and Hattie,' he said. 'It must be time for you to go now. We will see you again soon.'

And, with that, he and all the other dragons sent them on their journey, wrapped in a warm blanket of smoke.

Mith Ickle led the way out of Dragon's Valley with Hattie following. The pink dragon didn't say anything, but Hattie could tell by how quiet she was that she was still upset. Hattie was glad they were on their way, but she didn't feel right without Mith Ickle curled comfortingly round her shoulders.

Once they had left the valley, Hattie had to consult the map again. The path seemed quite clear, but when they arrived at what should have been the Frozen Merlakes all Hattie could see was a solid wall of water looming ahead of them. It wasn't like the waterfalls Hattie had seen on holidays in the countryside with her family. There was no rushing, gushing water hurtling noisily downwards. Instead, the water ran down in a smooth silent sheet, like a giant piece of transparent paper.

'What do we do? Can we pass through?' Hattie asked Mith Ickle. She couldn't believe they had come so far to fail now.

'We can pass,' Mith Ickle said, scowling at the waterfall.

'I guess dragons don't like getting wet then?' Hattie asked her friend. 'Here – come close, Mith, and I'll try to keep you as dry as possible.'

Hattie's heart lifted when she saw Mith Ickle's expression soften, but the little dragon still huffed and puffed as she fluttered on to

Hattie's shoulders, hiding under the curtain of her hair.

'I hope the water's not too cold!' called Hattie as she prepared to run forward. Mith Ickle didn't answer, though Hattie noticed that her eyes had grown wide and her wings had risen slightly in anticipation. 'Let's go through on three. One . . . two . . . three!'

The water wasn't warm, but it wasn't as icy as Hattie had expected. She and Mith Ickle quickly ran through it and emerged on the other side. Squeezing a long trickle of water from her thick dark hair, Hattie watched as steam rose from Mith Ickle's small, hot body.

'That wasn't so bad, was it?' Hattie asked, but the dragon simply replied by snorting a puff of smoke crossly from both nostrils.

Leaving Mith Ickle to dry off in peace, Hattie began to look around her. On the frost-covered grassy edges of the lakes, Hattie spotted her first-ever mermaids. They were as beautiful as described in the books she'd read – long glossy hair that they continually brushed, perfect porcelain complexions, and faces that film stars in her world would do anything for – but, underneath it all, Hattie could sense the kind of hostility that made some pretty people not very pretty at all.

Hattie shivered and even Mith Ickle fluttered

closer to her. Where was the hidden lake and how were they meant to find it? She couldn't see anything from where she was. Taking a very careful step forward, she heard her trainers crunch on the frozen ground.

'What do you want, human?' hissed one of the mermaids suddenly, without even pausing to stop combing her long blonde hair.

'I . . . we're looking for the . . . the hidden l-lake,' stuttered Hattie, not sure if her teeth were chattering from the cold or from nerves. Her unease certainly didn't improve when the other mermaids began to snigger and whisper to each other.

'Should we tell her?' sneered a mermaid with curly red hair.

'No. Why should we? She'll never make it out anyway,' added a dark-haired mermaid sitting beside her. A tinkle of cold laughter echoed around the lake.

Realizing they were going to get no help from the mermaids, Hattie stumbled on, trying not to let their mean attitude get to her, though she was not quite sure where she and Mith Ickle were going. They passed snowberry bushes, went round a winter willow tree and, with Hattie taking care not to slip, crossed a crystal-clear ice bridge. It was on the other side of the bridge that Hattie stopped, feeling like they might blindly wander through the Frozen Merlakes forever.

Suddenly Mith Ickle flew up high. 'Stop, Hattie! Look!' Her musical voice filled the air.

'What?' asked Hattie, her eyes screwed up against the brightness of the sun. 'I can't see anything. It's so bright!'

'Exactly!' said Mith Ickle. 'The sun is at its very highest. Just as Themis said it should be.'

Hattie spun round in desperation. If the sun was at its highest . . .

She stopped in her tracks. Back on the other side of the bridge they'd just crossed was a wall of leaves that Hattie hadn't seen before. The leaves – some long and thin, others short and wide — were in bright shades of rich green, red, gold and brown. What really stood out, though, was the golden light that shone through them. A light so magical it could only be caused by the reflection from —

'Water!' Hattie cried. 'It must be the hidden lake!'

'Then we must go through to it as quickly as we can,' replied Mith Ickle.

Hattie smiled at her friend gratefully. Running over the bridge, she stretched out both arms and began to push excitedly through the luscious leaves to the lake beyond.

A Dragon's Song

After the frostiness of the merlakes, Hattie was surprised at the difference on the other side of the leafy curtain. Grateful for the warmer air, she looked around, taking in the clearing that surrounded them. Lush, mossy green grass bordered the hidden lake. Small clumps of pretty flowers burst out of the grass here and there, their petals every shade of pink, purple, yellow and orange.

Hattie's trainers sank into the soft ground as she walked to the water's edge. The sun streaked through the thick leaf canopy that hung over the lake, casting a golden glow on the crystal-clear water below. Peering into it, Hattie spotted small brightly coloured fish flitting about. She couldn't believe how beautiful this place was.

A rustle from a flower-laden bush behind Hattie brought her attention away from the beauty of the lake and she spun round just in time to see a flash of blue rushing towards her.

'What –' started Hattie. But, before she

could finish, she felt Mith Ickle swoop down in front of her and shoot out a huge burst of fire. The blue flash stumbled and Hattie saw that it was Immie.

The blue-haired imp backed away from Mith Ickle warily. 'Saved by a dragon – again!' she sneered nastily. 'You really don't have any other friends, do you, Hattie?'

Hattie ignored her. She'd learned to stand up to people like Immie just as she had with the mean girls in her class. Hattie knew who her real friends were.

'At least I have friends, Immie!' Hattie moved closer to Mith Ickle protectively. 'What do you have?'

Immie scowled. 'I'll tell you what I have, Hattie Bright. I have the magical moonstone.' She smirked and held up her palm. In it lay a beautiful, smooth, egg-shaped stone. It was a shade of ivory that glimmered with different coloured light from the very heart of it. It was mesmerizing.

'Give it back. Lunar needs it much more than you,' Hattie said, walking towards Immie with determination. But Immie wasn't about to give in.

'You can't make me,' she said, as she took a step back. 'Neither you nor your dragon *friend*.'

Hattie glanced at Mith Ickle to see how she

would react to Immie's remark. But, instead of blowing fire at the snippy imp, Mith Ickle broke into a melodious and enchanting song.

At first Hattie couldn't understand what her friend was doing, but then something she had learned from her last visit came back to her. With a grin she remembered how dragons use their song to lull their enemies into a deep sleep.

Hattie watched as Immie first closed her eyes, and then began to rock gently as sleep came over her. As she fell into a heavy slumber, Immie's arms dropped to her sides, her fingers uncurled and the moonstone fell and tumbled across the mossy grass beside her.

'Nooooooo!' cried Hattie in horror as she and Mith Ickle watched the precious stone roll quickly along the grass and disappear into the deep water of the lake with a loud *SPLASH*.

For a moment Hattie and Mith Ickle were too shocked to move, but Hattie soon raced to the water's edge, Mith Ickle flapping alongside. They both peered into the water but the moonstone was nowhere to be seen.

'It'll be right on the bottom,' said Hattie sadly, remembering how quickly Mrs Riley's yellow rings had sunk to the bottom of the pool at Swimming Club. 'How on earth are we going to find it again?'

Hattie knew the answer to her question as soon as she had asked it: someone would have to dive down into the lake and look for it.

Almost at once, Hattie felt the knot of nerves form in her stomach again. She could see that the sun wasn't going to stay at the highest point in the sky for long. If the sun disappeared, it would plunge the leafy clearing into darkness again. She also remembered that Mith Ickle really did not like getting wet. Hattie knew that she was the one who would have to dive.

At the lake's edge, Hattie stood trembling, her heart thumping hard in her chest. Even the warmth of Mith Ickle's body, as the little dragon curled round her shoulders, couldn't comfort her.

'We don't have much time,' whispered Mith Ickle, her warm breath brushing over Hattie's ear. 'Are you ready to jump in?'

'I don't know,' replied Hattie, her voice cracking with fear. 'I'm not very good at diving.'

'Just think about poor Lunar and how pleased you'll be when you've helped him to get better,' said Mith Ickle reassuringly.

Hattie glanced over at the still-sleeping Immie as Mith Ickle fluttered off her shoulders. 'You're right, Mith Ickle,' she said.

With that, she raised both arms above her head, took the deepest breath she could . . . and dived in.

Immie Learns a Lesson

Underwater, Hattie fought off the feeling of panic in order to keep kicking until she reached the very bottom of the lake. The water was so clear, and the moonstone so bright, that it didn't take her long to find the precious stone. Grabbing it tightly, she pushed herself back to the surface of the lake and gasped as she drew in air.

Wiping her wet hair away from her face, Hattie spotted Mith Ickle waiting anxiously at the water's edge, Immie still fast asleep beside her.

'I got it!' called Hattie with a smile, before glimpses of movement in the bushes caught her eye. She shivered as she remembered Themis's warning that the hidden lake was a dangerous place when it was dark. A glance up at the sky told her that the sun was definitely moving away from the clearing, which was beginning to cast a shadow over the lake. Hattie pulled herself out of the water quickly.

'Shall I breathe out some fire to dry you?' asked Mith Ickle, watching water slide down Hattie's face and body.

'I'm not sure we've got time,' replied Hattie, taking another look at the sky. 'It'll be dark soon, and those creatures Themis warned us about are already stirring — and it looks like Immie might be too!'

Hattie was right. With a cross *humph*, Immie got up and glared at Hattie, who couldn't resist giving the imp a glimpse of the moonstone that she now held.

Knowing she'd been beaten, Immie turned her back on Hattie and Mith Ickle and stomped away from them. She had barely taken two steps when a loud voice echoed across the sky, stopping the imp in her tracks and making Hattie and Mith Ickle jump in surprise.

'STOP, IMP! YOU HAVE FAILED ME AGAIN, USELESS SERVANT!' boomed the voice.

Hattie knew at once it could only come from one creature – King Ivar. Shaking nervously, Hattie felt Mith Ickle curl round her shoulders as Ivar's cackling voice filled the air again.

'NOW I'LL HAVE TO TAKE CARE OF THIS MYSELF – THE GUARDIAN MUST NOT SUCCEED. THE CREATURES OF BELLUA MUST BE UNDER MY POWER!'

Before Hattie could prepare herself for what Ivar might do next, a huge bang shook the air and a dark shadow filled the sky. Hattie looked up, bewildered, but Mith Ickle had a much better idea of what Ivar had in store for them.

'The shadow fairies are coming!' she called, her sing-song voice breaking with fear. 'They're the most mischievous fairies of all! They'll swarm over us within moments and we'll never get out of here. Quick, Hattie, we need to take cover now!'

Glancing around, Hattie spotted a flash of blue disappearing into a small bush just behind her. It was clear Immie knew exactly what was coming their way!

Mith Ickle began darting around wildly, looking for cover. Hattie's heart raced as she failed to see anywhere obvious to run to. Suddenly she noticed a bush laden with small berries, their brilliant green colour still glowing brightly in the shadowy air.

'Stinkberries!' she yelled at Mith Ickle. 'Quick, gulp some down. That pong should keep the shadow fairies away – it's got to be worth a try!'

Grabbing a handful of berries from the bush, Hattie quickly pushed a couple into her mouth. But as she held some out towards Mith Ickle she saw with horror that it was too late. A small group of fairies had already followed the little dragon, whose poor face was twisted in terror as they tugged mercilessly at her long pink tail, tormenting her and buzzing around her face.

'Get off her!' Hattie cried, running towards her friend.

It was only as she got closer that she realized the stinkberries must have already taken effect.

Wrinkling up their mischievous little noses, the shadow fairies began to cough and splutter, pinching their tiny nostrils together and darting away from her.

'It's working, it's working!' Hattie called excitedly. 'Here, Mith, eat these – the smell should get rid of the fairies in no time.'

Hattie held out the final few stinkberries she'd gathered and Mith Ickle quickly grabbed them, stuffing them into her mouth gratefully. Hattie was surprisingly delighted to find that Mith Ickle soon smelled as revolting as she did, and it wasn't long before the last of the shadow fairies squealed with disgust and left the poor dragon alone.

'Oh, Hattie, those berries were a great idea – well done!' Mith Ickle fluttered on to her friend's shoulder and nuzzled her gratefully.

'I'm just glad you're OK,' replied Hattie. 'But it looks like someone else might not be,' she added with a laugh, as she spotted the swarm of fairies heading towards the very bush that Immie had taken refuge in.

It wasn't long before the blue-haired imp emerged from the bush, batting wildly at the group of fairies who were tugging at her clothes, her hair and even her feet.

'Get off! Get off!' she cried angrily. 'Leave me alone, you horrid creatures!'

The fairies, however, had other ideas. Hattie

watched in amusement as Immie danced across the shadowy ground trying to shake them off, skipping all the way round the lake before disappearing through the leafy curtain.

'Come on, Mith. Let's follow her,' said Hattie, heading in Immie's direction.

Once through the leaf curtain, they were just in time to see Immie, still surrounded by fairies, at the edge of one of the merlakes. Too distracted, Immie failed to spot a mermaid's tail lying across the frozen ground. Hattie couldn't stop a small giggle escaping as she watched Immie trip over the tail and stumble a step or two before landing in the lake with a loud gasp and an even louder *SPLASH!*

The fairies soon scattered, avoiding the droplets of freezing water that flew up into the air. Taking one last disapproving sniff in the direction of Hattie and Mith Ickle, the troublesome creatures formed into one huge swarm and in seconds had flitted away from the merlakes completely, leaving a scowling Immie to climb soaking wet out of the water.

With the stench of the stinkberries lingering long enough to keep the fairies at bay, Hattie and Mith Ickle decided they had no time to waste in getting back to Lunar. Running away from the Frozen Merlakes, they headed towards Dragon's Valley, dashing through it and calling out a hurried hello to any dragons they passed

on their way. They both realized there was no time to stay – Lunar would be waiting anxiously for them to return, his injured horn causing him to grow weaker. Mith Ickle gave Hattie a reassuring nudge with her little scaly nose to make sure that her friend knew she didn't mind not stopping with the dragons.

Rushing as much as they could, Hattie and Mith Ickle soon found themselves passing under the ornate arch that welcomed them back to Unicorn Meadows. They weren't surprised to see Themis and the other unicorns waiting for them.

'We welcome your swift return, Hattie,' said

Themis, before nodding to a large dapple-grey unicorn standing just behind him. 'Dusk will speed you to our injured friend Lunar. This will hasten the cure that may return magic to him and all of Bellua.'

Before Hattie could say anything, Dusk stepped forward and lowered his head so that Hattie could clamber on to a unicorn's neck for the second time that day.

Hattie wanted to reach Lunar as quickly as possible, before Ivar had a chance to cause trouble again. As she smiled gratefully at the head unicorn for everything he had done for her, she felt herself being lifted gracefully up into the air on Dusk's back.

With Dusk travelling effortlessly through the shimmering sky, Hattie and Mith Ickle arrived at the cave entrance in record time.

Dusk lowered Hattie slowly and elegantly.

'Thank you,' she said, stroking the grey unicorn's neck.

'You are welcome, Guardian. We look forward to seeing you in these lands again.'

'I'll come whenever I am needed,' Hattie replied earnestly. 'I promise.'

As Dusk flew away, Hattie and Mith Ickle both ran to the cave door and hurried inside. Lunar was where they had left him, resting on the hard cave floor, his eyes dimmer than before. He tried to say hello, but his voice had weakened to barely a whisper.

'I have to make the healing paste as fast as I can,' said Hattie, placing the moonstone on the table. Next to it was the bottle of rainbow water that Mith Ickle had found before they set off. 'Now, what can I use that will be tough enough to crush this beautiful moonstone?'

Hattie looked along the shelves several times without finding anything useful. Then, at the very end of a shelf heaving with bottles, she found a small wooden box with one word written in neat capitals on its lid: DIAMONDS.

'This is what I need, Mith!' Hattie cried excitedly. 'My brother, Peter, once told me that diamond is the hardest material you can find; it'll even cut through glass.'

At the time Hattie hadn't been sure whether Peter was telling her the truth – like lots of big brothers, his favourite activity was teasing his younger sister — but she didn't know what other options she had. She had to give the diamonds a try.

Placing the moonstone in a small stone bowl with the diamonds, Hattie was pleased to find she could crush it more easily than she had thought. She even felt a grudging gratitude to Peter for telling her about diamonds. Although Hattie thought it a shame to destroy the beautiful pearly moonstone, one glance at the stricken Lunar told her that a healed unicorn horn was more precious than any stone.

Before Hattie mixed up the paste that she

hoped would cure Lunar, she knew there was something else she had to do. Reaching for an empty glass bottle on the cave shelves, she took a small pinch of the crushed moonstone and carefully dropped it inside. With a pen she'd found beside the bowl of vet's instruments, she wrote the word MOONSTONE on the bottle's label in her neatest writing. Then she returned the bottle to the shelf, where it joined the one full of sunray-flower petals.

Hattie felt a rush of pride on seeing two of her own bottles on the crowded shelves. She really felt that she had begun to earn her place as the latest Guardian of the magical Kingdom of Bellua.

Taking the tiny bottle of rainbow water in her claws, Mith Ickle perched on the stone table and tipped several drops into the bowl containing the crushed moonstone. Hattie reached for a small silver spoon from the bowl of instruments beside her, then stirred the two magical ingredients together. She watched in wonder as the stone and water became a sparkling paste, with glittery specks of gold and silver running through it.

Hattie carefully carried the bowl over to Lunar and knelt down beside him. She whispered soothingly to him as she gently spread the magical paste along the crack in his horn.

As soon as the bowl was empty, a flash of light came from the horn, which was now glowing so brightly that Hattie and Mith Ickle had to close their eyes. Gradually opening her eyes, Hattie saw that Lunar had got up and was standing proud and tall. His eyes shone brightly again and his healed horn was dazzling.

'I cannot thank you enough, Guardian,' said Lunar, his voice now strong and deep, 'but I must return to my blessing without delay. You should know, Hattie, that you will always be a friend of the unicorns – and you too, Mith Ickle.'

The little dragon gave a small snort of pleasure, but, before Hattie could reply, a beam of light shot towards her from Lunar's horn.

As the light faded, Hattie noticed a tiny crystal unicorn charm on the floor by her feet.

'Thank you, Lunar,' she said, picking up the charm and fixing it to her bracelet.

However, Lunar had already trotted out of the cave and was on his way back to Unicorn Meadows.

With Lunar cured, Hattie knew her visit to Bellua was coming to an end. Saying goodbye to Mith Ickle would never be easy. She adored her dragon friend and hated leaving her, but she was thrilled that her trip had been another success – and that King Ivar and Immie hadn't managed to stop her yet.

'You *will* be here next time I come, won't you?' said Hattie, stroking the warm pink scales on the little dragon's head.

Mith Ickle nodded as Hattie reached for her

sparkly vet's bag, which she had left in a corner of the cave.

Opening it and peering inside to start her tumble back home, Hattie laughed as she heard Mith Ickle call her final goodbye: 'See you soon, Hattie – and try to land on your feet next time!'

Making a Splash

Hattie had only just returned to her bed with a bounce when Mum poked her head round the door.

'I know you're always starving after Swimming Club, so tea won't be long,' she said. 'I've put some sausages under the grill.'

At first Hattie was confused. She'd been all

the way to Bellua and back, yet Mum seemed to think they'd only just got back from swimming. Hattie then remembered how no time had passed in the real world when she'd last visited Bellua. She couldn't tell Mum about Bellua because she was bound by an ancient oath that meant she wasn't allowed to speak to anyone about the magical land. Except for Uncle B, of course. Hattie couldn't wait to see him again so she could tell him all about her adventures. She knew only he would really understand.

'Great! Thanks, Mum,' she replied, quickly pushing the vet's bag, now dull and battered again, under her bed. 'Call me when it's ready and I'll come straight down.'

The next day at school, Hattie's class had a swimming gala. The poolside seats were filled with friends and family who had come to watch. Remembering her best friend's tears the day before, Chloe had given Hattie's arm a reassuring squeeze as they'd left the changing room. Although Hattie was still dreading getting back into the water, she made sure to give Chloe a grateful smile in response, to let her know how much she appreciated her friendship and advice.

After gingerly lowering herself into the pool, Hattie did a couple of warm-up lengths with the others. Then Mrs Riley lined up all the girls in teams of four to swim a relay race. The first two girls in Hattie's team – Chloe and a shy girl called Lauren – swam their lengths in record time and Hattie watched nervously as the third swimmer, a small blonde girl called Georgia, dived in to take her turn. Hattie's stomach began churning with the thought that it would be her turn next. It didn't help that the team next to theirs had Victoria Frost and her two sidekicks, Jodie and Louisa – and that Victoria was also waiting to take her turn in the race.

'I don't think Hattie's team will be much competition,' Hattie heard Victoria say to her friends, her whisper deliberately loud enough for everyone to hear. 'I mean, all *four* team members have to actually dive in and swim, if they want to be in with a chance of winning.'

Hattie began to tremble with fear and hurt. By the time Georgia was just a few strokes away, she wondered if there was any hope of proving Victoria wrong.

'It's nearly your turn,' Chloe whispered to Hattie, before noticing her friend's distraught face. 'Oh, Hattie, you don't have to do it, you know. I mean it's just a race. You don't have to prove anything to *her*,' Chloe continued, turning to glare at a smug-looking Victoria, who was still sniggering at the side of the pool.

Hattie looked at Georgia swimming steadily towards her, then at the friendly faces of Chloe and Lauren. Could she do it? For herself and her teammates — just like she'd rescued the moonstone for Lunar? For a moment Hattie wasn't sure, but, as Georgia's fingertips touched the end of the pool, she felt the fluttery feeling disappear from her tummy. A vision of the beautiful hidden lake flashed in front of her and Hattie stretched her arms high above her head, arched her body and dived in.

It wasn't the best dive she had ever done, but when Hattie rose to the water's surface she felt a huge grin spread across her face as the cheers of her teammates and the crowd of spectators echoed down the pool. Kicking her legs as hard as she could, she powered towards the shallow end. Once there, she did a neat turn that sent her back towards the deep end and her final length.

It was only when Hattie was a few strokes from the finish line that she realized Victoria was swimming almost alongside her. Hattie knew there were only centimetres between her and Victoria, but she had never felt so determined!

Desperate to prove her mean classmate wrong, Hattie kicked her legs harder than ever. Could she manage to get just far enough ahead to win? With the end of the race in sight, Hattie sneaked a quick look to her side. She was ahead by at least a couple of strokes!

With a final kick, Hattie reached one arm towards the pool edge and felt the smooth tiles

under her fingertips. She'd dived in, swum faster than she'd ever swum before – *and* beaten Victoria Frost too!

The cheers from Hattie's teammates were still echoing around the pool when Victoria finished the race a few seconds later. Everyone at the poolside watched as she raised her head from the water. With an angry squeal, Victoria punched a fist into the water, sending a splash flying up in the air – and all over her scowling face. Victoria sulkily pulled herself out of the pool, before huffing all the way to the changing room without a word.

Back on the poolside, Hattie pushed her damp hair out of her face and wondered if she'd ever felt happier. Scanning the crowd, she spotted her mum and dad who were clapping with pride. Standing next to them with a big smile on his face was Uncle B – he'd come to watch her too! She flushed with pride as he gave her a knowing wink.

'See, you're great at diving, Hattie,' said Chloe, giving her best friend a hug. 'Cool swimming too!'

'I didn't want to let my team down,' replied Hattie, realizing that she could be as brave as anyone when those she cared about depended on her. She longed to tell Chloe about how she'd dived into the hidden lake to get the moonstone that had helped Lunar, but one

glance at Uncle B reminded Hattie of her oath of secrecy. The tales of unicorns and dragons and wicked imps had to stay in the magical kingdom where they belonged – for now.

'Come on, Chloe,' she said instead, linking her arm through her best friend's. 'Let's go and get changed.'

This time, there were no tears as Hattie got dressed. As she carefully put on her charm bracelet, the new unicorn charm glinted in the light.

When will I next be called back to Bellua? Hattie wondered.

For now, she would just have to wait and see, but one thing Hattie knew for sure – she

was ready and waiting to dive into her next adventure and face any challenge from King Ivar as soon as the tiny charms glowed.

Hattie's Journal

The creatures I discovered today

Dragon – I met lots today! But the most special of all was Mith Ickle. Tiny, pink, friendly and fiercely protective. I think we're going to be great friends.

Unicorn – tall and majestic. His coat was pure white and his mane was lilac. He was the leader of the other unicorns and his name was Themis.

Troll – lots of different shapes and sizes but all quite ugly and grumpy. I wonder if they have a secret sense of humour?

Imp – tiny with blue hair in bunches and pointy ears. Very pretty but mean. Well, this imp Immie was. Maybe the others are nicer?

Join Hattie in her next adventure in
The Fairy's Wing

There's no time to lose when Hattie B is called back to the Kingdom of Bellua. King Ivar of the Imps has decided he wants to fly, so he's taken the magic from a fairy's wing.

Hattie must find an enchanted thread to fix the wing, but someone is determined to stop her . . .

www.worldofhattieb.com

Dot-to-Dot

Join the dots to find the charm from Hattie's bracelet.

Hattie B
Magical Vet

Find out more about

Hattie B

and the creatures

from the

Kingdom of

Bellua

by visiting

www.worldofhattieb.com